YOU C...

LITTLE
MERMAID

AN INTERACTIVE
FAIRY TALE ADVENTURE

written by *Eric Braun*
illustrated by *Mariano Epelbaum*

CAPSTONE PRESS
a capstone imprint

You Choose Books are published by Capstone Press, an imprint of Capstone.
1710 Roe Crest Drive
North Mankato, Minnesota 56003
www.capstonepub.com

Library of Congress Cataloging-in-Publication data is available on the Library of
Congress website.
ISBN 978-1-5435-9013-5 (library binding)
ISBN 978-1-4966-5813-5 (paperback)
ISBN 978-1-5435-9017-3 (eBook PDF)

Summary: Readers navigate their way through three twisted versions of the classic
fairy tale "The Little Mermaid."

Editorial Credits
Editor: Michelle Parkin; Designer: Brann Garvey; Media Researcher: Eric Gohl;
Production Specialist: Kathy McColley

All internet sites appearing in back matter were available and accurate when this book
was sent to press.

Printed and bound in the USA.
PA100

TABLE OF CONTENTS

ABOUT YOUR ADVENTURE

Life inside your sleepy little town is safe and predictable. But is that what you want? Adventure, mystery, and maybe even a little danger await you outside the city limits. Do you want to be part of that world?

In this fairy tale, you control your fate. Go under the sea and make choices to determine what happens next.

Chapter One sets the scene. Then you choose which path to read. Follow the directions at the bottom of the page as you read the stories. The decisions you make change your outcome. After you finish one path, go back and read others for new perspectives and more adventures.

PART OF YOUR WORLD

YOU live in a small but charming town called Waterville. Everyone is happy here. And why not? It is beautiful. There are old brick buildings and houses with vines growing on them. Towering trees and colorful flowers sway in the breeze. Birds of all types fill the air, flitting from tree branch to tree branch and settling on people's windowsills. The sky is especially beautiful—a swirling blue that almost looks as if it is water. Everyone here knows one another, and most everyone gets along.

Your house is a lovely old building at the edge of the forest. You live there with your father and five brothers and sisters. Your mother died years ago. Your grandmother also lives with you. She is a proud old woman who always wears twelve pearls in her hair. You and your siblings share a beautiful garden, which you spend lots of time in.

Life is simple and comfortable. But you are restless. Everyone around you is happy, but you are not. You have always wanted something more from life. You long for adventure. You just know a more exciting world is out there. There has to be! The problem is, your father won't let you leave town until you're older. Until then, you have to wait.

Year after year, your brothers and sisters grow up and leave to explore the outside world. Each one returns with wonderful stories about art, adventure, sports, and food. But after their travels, each one decides to stay home with family. The world is interesting, but home is where they belong.

Finally, you are old enough to leave town. What will you do on your adventure?

To sing in a band, turn to page 11.
To hang out with the rich and famous, turn to page 43.
To follow a fishy friend under the sea, turn to page 75.

CHAPTER 2

THE LITTLE ROCK STAR

You have loved music all your life. You started singing when you were young. It's your dream to be the lead singer in a great rock band, playing for big crowds.

You practice every day—in the shower, outside in your garden, on your way to school. And all your practice has paid off. You're a great singer. When people hear you, they swoon. In fact, you are the best singer in Waterville. Now that you've finally left town, you're excited to make your dreams come true.

The first night in the city, you go to a rock concert by the most famous band around—The Humans. It is amazing! You dance and sing along to your favorite songs.

After the show, you head outside to wait for your cab. Suddenly a crowd of fans comes rushing toward you.

"There they are!" screams a woman you recognize from the concert.

"Can I get a selfie with you?!" cries a man wearing a T-shirt of the band.

You realize that The Humans are right behind you, getting into their tour bus. When the crowd catches up to you, it feels like you are getting washed up in a big ocean storm. You are pushed along by the wave of people. You land with a *THUD!* into some bushes.

This would never happen in Waterville, you think, pulling leaves from your hair.

You look up and see the tour bus slowly driving through the crowd. As you start to stand, you hear someone groaning in pain. There in the bushes is Joey Prince, the lead guitarist of The Humans. He must have been knocked out by the force of the surging crowd. Nobody noticed that he fell back here.

You pull the hood of his sweatshirt down over his face. If this crowd sees him, who knows what they would do. Joey moans. You notice his head is bleeding. You take out your phone to call 9-1-1, but the battery is dead.

There's only one thing to do—you have to get Joey back to the band. Keeping his face covered, you drag Joey toward the bus. You make it to the door and bang loudly.

Someone inside looks out the bus window. He meets you at the door and pulls Joey inside.

"He's hurt," you say.

"Yeah, thanks," the man says. "Now move aside." He slams the door in your face.

The bus lurches and drives away, its red taillights twinkling in the dark night. Your own ride back to your hotel feels like a dream.

The next morning, you read online that The Humans are auditioning new members for the band. This is your chance! Maybe if Joey remembers you saved him, you'll have an edge over the competition.

15

Turn the page.

The day of the audition, you head downtown to Gold Tower Studios. There's a big turnout. Hundreds of people showed up to play or sing for The Humans. The band's manager, Mr. Seawitch, stands outside a large auditorium. You recognize him as the man who opened the bus door for Joey.

When you get to the front of the line, he doesn't recognize you. He looks at your simple clothes and laughs.

"You don't look like rock-star material," he says. "Next!"

"But wait!" you say. "I can sing."

"So can most of the people here," the manager says, pointing to the huge crowd.

To sing and prove how good you are, go to page 17.
To find another way in the auditorium, turn to page 19.

Mr. Seawitch is guarding the door to the auditorium. There's no other way to get to the band. Maybe if you show the manager what a great singer you are, he'll let you in.

The grumpy manager is pointing toward the door, waiting for you to leave. Instead, you start singing your best song, "Sandcastle Love." It doesn't sound as good without a guitar, but you are sure he will be impressed.

Mr. Seawitch is annoyed at first, but then his expression changes. His eyes turn soft. You finish the song.

"Very nice," he says.

"Thank you," you say. "So can I go try out for Joey and the rest of the band?"

Turn the page.

"I'm afraid not," Mr. Seawitch says. "My daughter wants to be their new singer. There is only one spot available. I won't risk you getting it instead of her. So you're staying right here."

"Great voice, though," he adds. "You have a real future—somewhere else."

What now? You can feel your future slipping away.

To try out for another spot in the band, turn to page 20.
To run for the auditorium door, turn to page 24.

"Okay, fine," you say with a huff.

You leave through the lobby. Outside, people are bustling to work or talking on their phones. Some are drinking coffee. You sit on a bench to think.

There's got to be a way to get to the band, you think.

You get up and start to walk. You go down an alley near the studio. That's when you notice the band's tour bus parked along the side. You get an idea.

You walk to the bus and try the door. It's unlocked! What luck. Nobody is on board, but the band has to get on eventually, right?

To climb onto the bus and wait, turn to page 28.
To look for a back door to the studio, turn to page 31.

"Wait! Wait!" you say as Mr. Seawitch tries to push you out the door. "I won't take your daughter's spot as singer. What else is available?"

Mr. Seawitch checks his clipboard. "We're looking for a violinist too."

You don't stop to think. "I can do that! Please, will you let me play for them?"

Mr. Seawitch shakes his head. "Right. I let you in and you start singing. You're not tricking me."

"I promise," you say.

"I have a better idea," Mr. Seawitch says. He goes into a back room and returns with a big bottle of hot sauce. "Drink this."

"Drink hot sauce?" you ask. "Why?"

"It has some of the hottest peppers around," he says. "You won't be able to sing a note."

You grab the bottle and open it. Fiery fumes instantly go up your nose. Your eyes water.

"Go on," he says.

You lift the bottle to your mouth and start to drink. You only get a little bit down before you have to stop. You start coughing.

"All of it," Mr. Seawitch orders.

It takes several tries, but you get all of the hot sauce down. Your eyes continue to water. Your forehead and neck are dripping with sweat. Your throat feels like someone ran a cheese grater over it.

"Now let me in," you whisper. Your voice is so cracked and weak, you can barely hear yourself.

Mr. Seawitch keeps his promise. He hands you a violin and opens the door to the room where the band is gathered.

You wave to Joey Prince as you walk in. He looks at you kindly but doesn't seem to recognize you.

"You can start playing whenever you're ready," Joey tells you.

You look down at the violin in your hands. What have you gotten yourself into? Sure, your brother taught you how to play, but that was ages ago.

With all eyes on you, you can barely remember your name, let alone how to play this thing. You realize that you have very little chance of getting into the band as a violinist. But this is your only shot. You have to do something.

23

To try to play a song on the violin, turn to page 33.
To try talking to Joey Prince, turn to page 35.

If there is one thing you're good at, it is singing. And the band is *right there*. If you don't sing now, you will never get another chance. You take a deep breath and run for the auditorium.

"Hey, stop right there!" you hear Mr. Seawitch shout. "Security!"

Just as you reach the door, a security guard grabs you by the sleeve. He tries to pull you away.

"No!" you cry.

As you are being led away, you start to sing "Nothing but Bubbles." You sing as loudly as you can to the closed auditorium door. You sound amazing. But can the band hear you? Suddenly, the door opens. Joey Prince and the rest of The Humans stand in the doorway.

"Stop it!" Mr. Seawitch yells. "I'm sorry, Mr. Prince, I told her tryouts were over."

"It's okay," Joey says. "She's good. Let her sing."

You finish your song in the hallway. When you're done, everyone claps—everyone except Mr. Seawitch.

"Come on in," Joey says, pointing to the auditorium. "I'd like to hear more. We're also considering another singer, Lisa Seawitch."

You walk into the auditorium. Inside is a young woman standing by a microphone. You introduce yourself and shake hands. Joey tells you that Lisa will sing first. Then it will be your turn. You realize that this is a competition between the two of you. The winner will be the new lead singer of The Humans. The loser is going back home.

Turn the page.

Lisa begins to sing. You have to admit, she is not bad. The drummer closes his eyes and nods along. The bass player smiles. When she's finished, Lisa looks at you and winks.

Do you have what it takes to win? Suddenly, you're not so sure. You could use an extra edge. What if you sang a song about saving Joey from the crowd? He might remember you. That might be enough.

To make up a song about saving Joey, turn to page 37.
To sing one of your best songs, turn to page 39.

You know The Humans will get on the tour bus sooner or later. When they do, you'll be waiting. You will have to do some fast talking, but it's your best chance. You climb in and take a seat.

The bus stays empty for hours. You're bored and frustrated, but at least the tour bus is comfy. You spend the time curled up on a couch. Later that night, you hear the bus door open. You jump up from your seat, ready to sing your heart out. But it's not the band who climbs on board. It's their manager, Mr. Seawitch.

"Hey!" he says when he sees you. "You can't be in here!"

"I'm here to sing for the band!" you insist.

But Mr. Seawitch is not listening. Instead, he's on his phone calling the police. You realize you've made a big mistake. This just got serious.

You try to leave, but the manager is too fast. He gets off the bus and locks you inside.

"Oh, no you don't," he says through the closed door. "You're staying there until the police come."

Several minutes pass. You can hear Mr. Seawitch talking to The Humans about you. He won't let them on the bus until the cops have taken you away.

"Let me out of here!" you yell, banging on the door. But the band isn't listening.

"She's just another crazed fan," Mr. Seawitch says. "She's probably dangerous." **29**

The band members agree, and they wait outside. Soon the police arrive. You try to explain what you were doing there, but they're not listening either. The next thing you know, you are in the back of the squad car.

Later, you go in front of a judge. You're not going to jail, but you can't go near Joey Prince and The Humans. You won't be able to see them in concert, let alone join the band. You return home. You spend the rest of your days in Waterville, listening to The Humans on the radio.

THE END

To follow another path, turn to page 9.

Getting onto the bus is too risky. You want to join the band, not get arrested. So you continue walking down the alley. Several doors line the walls into the building. You try each one. Finally, you find one that's unlocked. You pull it open and go inside.

Right away, alarms go off. Mr. Seawitch and security appear in the hall.

"I told you to get out of here!" he says. The band comes into the hallway too.

"What's going on?" Joey Prince says.

"Joey!" you cry. "Do you remember the night you got hurt after the concert? I pulled you to safety!"

Joey shakes his head. "What are you talking about? My manager saved me that night."

Turn the page.

"No, it was me," you cry. "We were meant to meet that night. I'm supposed to be your new lead singer."

And with that, you belt out a powerful love song. Mr. Seawitch tries to stop you, but Joey lets you finish. When you're done, everyone tells you how great you were.

"That was beautiful," Joey says, "but we already found our new singer—Mr. Seawitch's daughter." He reaches into his pocket and pulls out a couple of concert tickets. "But hey, take these," Joey says. "It's a little out of the way, but it'll be a great show."

"Thanks," you mutter. Your heart is broken. You look at the tickets. The concert is in Waterville. You'll be going home after all.

THE END

To follow another path, turn to page 9.

You decide to play a song on the violin. What choice do you have? Your bow squeals along the strings. It sounds terrible, but you push your way through it. When you finish, you look up at your audience. They stare at you in disbelief.

"Well," says Joey Prince, faking a smile. "Thanks for coming in. Don't call us. I mean, we'll call you if we need you."

"Could I try singing a song?" you croak. But it's obvious your voice is shot. "Never mind."

You return home to Waterville. You are sad and angry for weeks. You never leave your room. Then one day, your grandmother knocks on your bedroom door.

"Come in," you say. Your grandmother walks in, holding a guitar in her hand.

Turn the page.

"I got you something," she says proudly. "Let's sign you up for guitar lessons."

You know that she is just trying to help, but the idea is ridiculous. Why would you ever want to play music again after what happened? You place the guitar at the end of your bed and get back to sulking.

Weeks later the guitar is still there, untouched. Tired of wallowing, you pick up the instrument and strum a few chords. You like it! You take the lessons and get better. Soon, you are playing with friends—a drummer and bass player. Forget about The Humans. You start your own band—The Mermaids!

THE END

To follow another path, turn to page 9.

You lift the violin to your chin, but then set it down. You walk to the desk where the band is sitting and grab a pen and some paper.

You write:

Joey, I can't play the violin. I sing, but I can't right now. I hope you give me another chance. And I have to tell you something. Do you remember the night the crowd stormed your tour bus?

"Of course," Joey Prince replies, reading the note. "It was a terrible night."

You continue to write:

I was there. I helped you get to the bus.

"Liar!" Mr. Seawitch shouts, reading over Joey's shoulder. "I am the one who saved you, Joey."

Turn the page.

"You do look familiar," Joey says to you.

Then someone else speaks up. "Are you guys ready to practice?" It's a girl over by the microphone.

"Yes," Joey says. Then he turns to you. "I'm sorry, but I don't remember you. And even if I did, we're not looking for a singer anymore. If you can't play the violin, we have nothing open for you."

You feel your face turn hot. Your hands turn cold. You realize you won't get your chance to sing in front of Joey. You will never be part of this world.

THE END

To follow another path, turn to page 9.

Lisa sounded amazing. The band loved it, you could tell. You need every advantage you can get.

When it's your turn to sing, you make up lyrics on the spot. You have an amazing voice, so it's okay if the song is not as polished. The important thing is to get the story out.

"The show that night was great," you sing. "Then the crowd couldn't wait. They had to meet you, a storm did greet you, and then I found you. You had on a hood . . . um, hold on, what rhymes with *hood?*"

Everyone is staring at you. You sing, "I felt like you understood!" You're so excited about the rhyme that you yell it out, your voice hitting a screeching pitch. "Oh, sorry," you say. "Let me start over."

37

Turn the page.

"That's okay," Joey says, holding up a hand. "I think we've heard enough."

"No, wait! This is just a new song. I've got it now." You start to sing louder. "I knew we were a good fit, when I grabbed you by the armpit!"

"Come on," Mr. Seawitch says, shaking his head. He leads you to the door.

The band hires Lisa as their singer. Every time you hear them on the radio, it reminds you of your horrible audition.

Did I really sing about Joey Prince's armpit? you think to yourself.

You shake your head. You wish you would have just trusted your talent.

THE END
To follow another path, turn to page 9.

Lisa is really good. When she finishes singing, all the band members clap loudly.

"Wow!" Joey says.

"Wonderful!" the drummer exclaims.

You remain calm. Yes, she is good. But you believe in yourself. Now it's your turn. You choose "Mermaid Tears." It's one of your favorite songs. You close your eyes and begin to sing. The melody fills the auditorium. You can feel everyone's emotions surrounding you and lifting you up.

When you finish, the auditorium is silent. You open your eyes and look around. Did you blow it? Why isn't anyone clapping? Finally, Joey Prince breaks the silence.

"I've never heard anyone sing like that," he says. "That was incredible."

The band hires you to be their new singer. Mr. Seawitch quits in protest. You start practicing right away. A few months later, it's time for your first concert together. You are amazing!

The band's popularity soars. The Humans' concerts attract bigger and bigger crowds.

You love being a rock star, and it turns out you're great at it. You spend the rest of your life traveling the world, playing to huge audiences, and writing new songs with your best friend, Joey Prince. You even get to play a few shows in Waterville in front of your family and friends.

But no matter where you play, you always follow one important rule: When a big crowd storms the parking lot, you stay on the bus!

THE END

To follow another path, turn to page 9.

CHAPTER 3

BE CAREFUL WHAT YOU WISH FOR

You come from a family of gardeners. Your grandmother taught you how to dig in the soil and grow beautiful flowers. Your father is an expert botanist. Your siblings have been looking for gardening jobs, but opportunities are scarce.

You love gardening too. You hope to make a career out of it. You imagine making floral masterpieces in the gardens of wealthy clients. Your creations will be known worldwide. It is almost magical how your touch makes gardens thrive. They bloom before your eyes.

Your family is poor, but at least you have each other. It is the same for most people in Waterville. No one you know is rich. Ah, but you have heard of the wealthy class. They live lavish lifestyles, with fancy cars and stylish clothes. Your siblings have seen their manicured lawns and sprawling landscapes on their way to work.

The rich have parties in big mansions with live music. Waiters serve them food on silver platters. You imagine what their beautiful and happy lives must be like. They probably laugh all the time, because they never have anything to worry about. They can afford to buy everything they want. Not like you and your family.

"I wonder what it would be like to be part of that world?" you say to yourself.

On the night of your birthday, you decide to find out. You travel to Cash Valley. It is where many rich people live. You walk the town and see wealthy people everywhere. One man wears a diamond-encrusted hat. A woman wears giant pearls in her hair.

Suddenly a clap of thunder shakes the sky. Rain begins to pour down.

Time to stop people-watching, you think.

You dash into Sebastian's, the most popular restaurant in town. It took you months to get a reservation. You look at the menu. You've saved up your allowance but all you can afford is a lettuce leaf and a piece of bacon. But it doesn't matter. You are excited to be here.

A party is going on in another part of the restaurant. People are dancing. Money is practically falling out of their pockets.

It is a birthday party for one of the men. He wears a gold dinner jacket and has hair like a movie star. He cracks jokes, and everyone laughs. They all want to be around him. So do you.

Soon your plate is empty, and you pay your check. Before you leave, you stop at the bathroom. There in the hall, you see the man with the gold jacket.

"Happy birthday," you say.

He thanks you and introduces himself as Chauncey. When you shake hands, he sees the dirt under your fingernails. At first, you are embarrassed. You tell him that you are a gardener, and it's your birthday too.

"Happy birthday," Chauncey says. "You know, most people in Cash Valley look down their noses at gardeners. But I love the magic you do."

While his party goes on without him, Chauncey talks with you about roses and ritzy dinners, sandalwood and sports cars. When you finally leave, you know that this was the best part of your birthday. You hope he feels the same.

You leave the restaurant to find the storm is raging with fairy tale intensity. The streets are flooded. Rain comes down so hard, it's like you're underwater. You stand beneath the restaurant's awning to stay dry, but the water in the street keeps rising.

48 You are still standing there when Chauncey's party lets out. People step out into the current. A woman is swept away down the street. A man slips and goes under the water. Chauncey holds on to a light pole, but his grip is loosening.

To try to save Chauncey, go to page 49.
**To grab on to something before you're swept away,
turn to page 55.**

Chauncey is pulled down the street. You have to save him. You jump into the street and fight against the waves. The water is freezing. Your shoulder slams into a fire hydrant, but you keep going. A golden convertible floats past you like a dinghy. Expensive necklaces and earrings from a flooded jewelry store bob up and down amidst the bubbles.

Finally you catch up to Chauncey. The water's current took him straight into a street sign. He's unconscious. You grab Chauncey under the arm and get his face above the water. You swim toward a fancy shoe store and grab on to the side of the building. The rain keeps pelting you, but at least you're safe for now. Chauncey is still out cold, but he is breathing. You check his wallet and find his address on his driver's license. Then you grab Chauncey and swim him home.

Turn the page.

Chauncey lives in a grand mansion on a hill overlooking the town. When you get there, you drag him up the hill to safety. You bang on the front door, but nobody answers.

You take him around to the back of the house. There you notice the garden. You run your hand across the bark of a puny-looking tree. At your touch, it grows into a gorgeous evergreen. You set Chauncey against it. Just then, a light comes on inside. You know your friend will be found soon.

You return home to Waterville. You can't stop thinking about Chauncey and the night of the party. You go back to Cash Valley a few times to spy on Chauncey. At first, it was just to see if he was okay. But now, it's something more. You see that Chauncey is a generous person who has lots of friends. He treats everyone well, no matter their status.

One day, you tell your grandmother about your visits to Cash Valley. You tell her how much you want to be one of the wealthy residents. You love it there. But the more you visit, the sadder you get about your own life.

Your grandmother worries about you. She has a solution to your problem. She tells you about an old warlock who lives in the forest at the edge of town.

"He grants wishes," she says. "He may be able to help."

"He can make me rich?" you ask. "Thank you, Grandma. Thank you!" You are about to leave for the forest when your grandmother calls to you.

"Beware, my child," she warns. "Yes, the warlock grants what your heart desires. But his spells cost more than you think."

Turn the page.

Your grandmother's warning doesn't stop you. You walk until you reach the forest. But the closer you get to the warlock's house, the more you see signs of dark magic. The sky has turned from blue to jet black. Vultures circle overhead. Dead trees and plants line the path to the warlock's house. Everything smells rotted. As you walk by, a row of bushes comes to life. The thick branches reach out to you like fingers, trying to pull you in. Plants hiss at you like snakes. You dodge them and keep going.

Finally you get to the warlock's home. The leaning shack is made of gnarled branches and poisonous nettles.

"Warlock!" you call.

A moment later, a hunched old man opens the door. He has yellow skin and thin, ropey arms. He smells like rotten vegetables.

The warlock invites you inside. You tell him about your wish to live among the high society in Cash Valley.

"I can cast a spell that will make you rich," the warlock cackles. "But it will cost you something you love. You will never be able to garden again. For the rest of your life, every plant you touch will wither and die."

"When I'm rich, I can pay someone to garden for me," you say confidently.

"Ah, but there's more," the warlock warns. "Once you cross over to that world, you
54 must convince Chauncey to call you his best friend. If he doesn't, you will die like the flowers you touch."

To accept the warlock's offer, turn to page 58.
To go to Cash Valley without the spell, turn to page 62.

You're a good swimmer, but it's way too dangerous to dive into the rushing water. You grab on to a mailbox and hold on as tight as you can. The current pulls at you, but you don't let go. Suddenly Chauncey loses his grip. You helplessly watch as Chauncey floats away, thrashing in the choppy water.

After a long time, the storm starts to die down. You wade against the current until you get uphill to dry land. Finally, you make your way home. It's been a scary and soggy evening.

Some birthday, you think to yourself.

You dry yourself off with a towel and head straight to bed. The next morning, you read about the storm online. A picture of Chauncey's smiling face is at the top of the story.

Turn the page.

"Chauncey Richington drowned in last night's massive storm," your sister reads over your shoulder. "Huh. I guess he wasn't rich enough to afford swimming lessons!" She laughs and walks away.

But you don't laugh. You cry. Maybe you could have helped him. You decide that when you have enough money, you will go back to Cash Valley and Sebastian's. You want to honor Chauncey's memory.

After a few months, you've saved enough money to return to the fancy restaurant. You wear your nicest clothes and order your lettuce leaf and piece of bacon. Once again, there is a birthday party going on. On your way to the bathroom, you meet the birthday girl in the hall.

"Hi," you say cheerfully. "Happy birthday."

"Uh, thanks, I guess," she says. "Do I know you?"

You extend your hand to introduce yourself, but the woman is staring at your fingernails.

"I'm a gardener," you explain.

"Ew, gross," she says. "Don't touch me with that filthy hand. Maybe you should do your nails before you come to a place like this. Or at least wash them."

The woman storms off, and you are left standing there. You think about Chauncy and how nice he was. You had hoped to meet someone else like him, but that doesn't seem likely. You decide not to return to Cash Valley again. You don't fit in here. You never will.

THE END
To follow another path, turn to page 9.

"It's worth it," you tell the warlock. "I'm ready for my new life."

The warlock smiles a sinister grin. "We'll see," he mutters to himself.

The warlock hands you some strange herbs and tells you to put them in your pockets. Then he burns more herbs in the fireplace. The room fills with a deep-green smoke.

"Breathe it in," he says.

You kneel by the fireplace and inhale the smoke. It circles around you. It makes you cough until tears stream down your face. Soon you are coughing so hard that you throw up. You're very thirsty and begin to sweat. You try to stand, but you fall to your knees. Then you pass out.

When you wake up, the smoke is gone. You pick yourself up off the floor.

"What happened?" you ask the warlock, holding your head.

"The spell worked," the warlock says. "Now go. Make Chauncey your friend. Time is ticking."

As you walk out of the house, you feel something bulky in your pockets. You remember the herbs. You reach inside, but the herbs are gone. Instead there are huge wads of cash! You pull the money out and begin to count, but there's too much. Your pockets are overflowing!

You tuck the money back into your pockets and walk quickly through the dark forest. Along the way, you see a tree branch stretched across your path. You push it to the side. Suddenly, you hear an awful sizzling sound. You watch as the branch and the tree it's connected to turn dark black. The tree twists into a shriveled mess. Smoke rises off the dead plant.

You remember the price you paid to the warlock and shiver.

I don't want to end up like that, you think.

You head straight for Cash Valley and walk inside an expensive-looking store. You buy a whole new wardrobe. Then you get the most expensive haircut you have ever had. You make your way to Chauncey's house in your new car.

You knock on the door. A butler answers, and you ask to see Chauncey. When Chauncey comes down, you reintroduce yourself.

"Do you remember me?" you ask. "We met at your birthday party."

61

But Chauncey shakes his head.

To tell Chauncey you saved his life, turn to page 64.
To pretend to be a rich person, turn to page 66.

You turn down the warlock's offer. The price is too steep. You'll find another way to become one of Cash Valley's elite. The warlock might have been on to something when he told you to be friends with Chauncey. A rich best friend could be your way into that world.

But when you go to Chauncey's house, he doesn't remember you. You leave disappointed, but you're not ready to give up. Chauncey may not remember how you saved him, but that doesn't mean you can't be friends now.

That evening, you follow Chauncey when he leaves his house. He goes to a fancy restaurant with his friends. You take a seat next to him at the table.

Chauncey gives you a startled look and motions to the restaurant manager. You don't have a reservation, so you are asked to leave.

When Chauncey leaves the restaurant, you call to him. He doesn't even look at you.

You follow Chauncey and his friends to an outdoor concert. You push your way through the crowd and start to dance next to him.

"I love this band," you say as you dance around. Soon security comes up and asks to see your concert ticket. "I don't have one," you admit, and you are forced to leave.

Sitting alone on the curb, you start to mope. You realize you'll never belong in Cash Valley. The people here only care about money and popularity—two things you'll never have without the warlock's help. You walk home to Waterville feeling sorry for yourself.

THE END
To follow another path, turn to page 9.

"I met you in the hallway the night of your birthday party," you say. "We talked about gardens. You said you thought gardeners were magical." You continue, "After the party, I pulled you out of the water during the storm and took you home."

Chauncey looks at you for a moment, trying to recognize your face. Finally he shakes his head.

"I'm sorry, I don't remember. I was in shock. My friend Thurston was at my house when I got up. I thought he saved me."

"No, it was me," you say. You hope that he believes you.

"Well, thank you for saving me," Chauncey says with a smile. "Let me take you to lunch to show my appreciation."

You are on cloud nine. Chauncey takes you to one of the most exclusive restaurants in all of Cash Valley. While you're eating, a young man comes up to the table. It's Thurston. After lunch, the three of you hang out all afternoon.

You and Chauncey become fast friends. It's everything you imagined. You eat at fancy country clubs. You drive expensive sports cars. Chauncey introduces you to his fiancée, Buffy. She is kind and friendly. One day Buffy tells you that Chauncey plans to ask his best friend to be in the wedding. But she doesn't know who it is.

You remember what the warlock said. If Chauncey doesn't say you are his best friend, you will die. You need to think of a way to convince him to choose you.

To write a song for Chauncey and Buffy, turn to page 68.
To give them flowers for the wedding, turn to page 70.

Maybe it's a good thing Chauncey does not remember you. That means he doesn't know you're really a poor gardener. You decide to try impressing him with all of your money.

"Hey, let me buy you lunch," you say. "I can afford it." You show him the wads of cash in your pocket.

"Of course you can afford it," Chauncey says, laughing. "Everyone around here is rich."

During lunch, you brag about all the connections you have. "I can get us into the best clubs in the world. We could travel anywhere you want, Chauncey. Just say the word!"

But Chauncey looks uncomfortable. "Um, I barely know you," he says.

I'm trying too hard! you think. *I need to relax.*

But things never get better between you. Soon Chauncey looks at his phone.

"Well, would you look at the time," he says. "I . . . uh . . . have to meet a friend at the country club. Thanks for lunch."

"No, wait," you say. "I'll come with you."

But Chauncey leaves before you can stop him. He will never be your friend. As he walks away, you know you are done for. You can already feel your skin starting to dry. You run to the post office and mail the rest of your money to your family. At least they'll be able to use it.

THE END
To follow another path, turn to page 9.

You write a song about true love for Chauncey and Buffy. You practice all night. By morning, it sounds pretty good. You're excited to share it with them.

Later on, you meet Thurston and Chauncey. Everything seems to be going well until Chauncey turns to Thurston.

"Thurston, you've been in my life so long," Chauncey starts. "You are my very best—"

"Wait!" you interrupt. "I wrote a song for you and Buffy. I can sing it at the wedding."

"How delightful!" Chauncey says.

You play the song for him on the guitar, singing your heart out. When you finish, Chauncey has a tear in his eye.

"That was so sweet," he says. "You truly are my best friend."

"Yes!" you yell.

"Hey, what about me?" Thurston shouts.

But Chauncey has made up his mind. And with those words, you are safe from the warlock's spell. You attend the wedding as a special guest and perform your song.

Afterward, you buy a huge mansion with your money and move your whole family to Cash Valley. None of you ever have to work again. Your father still gardens, but it is for fun instead of a paycheck. You and your family live the rest of your lives in luxury.

THE END

To follow another path, turn to page 9.

Your family grows the best flowers in Waterville. That will be perfect for Chauncey's wedding. You tell Chauncey and Buffy that you will provide all the flowers for their big day. They couldn't be more thrilled.

The next day, you beg your father to give you all the flowers he has in the garden. He's reluctant—those flowers are for everyone. Your siblings sell them for extra money. Your grandmother looks at them from her bedroom window. But you persist. You have to have every single flower. Finally, your father agrees.

On the day of the wedding, your father prepares a stunning display. The wedding is practically alive with the colors of hundreds of gorgeous flowers. Guests can't stop commenting on how great they look. Chauncey and Buffy hug you.

The ceremony starts, and you take your seat. The bride and groom begin to exchange their vows. Suddenly, you notice one of the roses is out of place on the banister. You can't have that. This day has to be perfect. You bend down and fix it.

There, you think in satisfaction.

But the flower starts to turn black. It droops and falls to the ground. The curse! You are horrified to see a chain reaction has started. One after the other, the roses on the banister begin to wither and die around the bride and groom. Then the flowers on the other side of the row start to die. The flowers on the altar, on the tables, in the entryway . . . they all die.

Turn the page.

The guests gasp. Chauncey stops his vows and stares at the dead plants surrounding them. Then Chauncey and Buffy look at you.

"You've ruined everything!" Buffy cries. She runs out of the ceremony.

"Buffy, wait!" Chauncey calls. Then he turns to you. "You are no friend of mine. Get out of here!"

You leave in tears and collapse in a small garden outside the wedding. How could this have gone so wrong? Chauncey hates you. You know you will wither like all of those wedding flowers. You wish you had never made that deal with the warlock.

73

THE END
To follow another path, turn to page 9.

CHAPTER 4

UNDER THE SEA

Today is your birthday. But it is not a happy day for you. Unlike your siblings, you don't have any friends to celebrate with. You've always had trouble connecting with people your age. Sure, your family is kind and loving. But you long for a friend. You're convinced you'll never find one in Waterville. So you travel far away from home.

Eventually you find yourself on a beach. You walk out onto a spit of land that extends like a finger into the ocean. There, you sit on the rocks and let the sun soak into you. You close your eyes and listen to the crashing waves. After a while, you hear something else—something beautiful. It is faint, but it sounds like singing.

You sit up and look around, but you don't see anyone on the shore. Then you look out toward the ocean, far out in the rolling waves. You see something out in the water—or someone. The sun is setting, and the sky is a brilliant orange and red. The bright colors make it hard to see, but it's definitely there.

You shade your eyes with your hand and stare out into the ocean. Yes, there's a girl about your age in the water. And she's singing. She swims closer when she sees you. She seems to be singing directly to you. She smiles and dives beneath the water. Then she comes up and leaps into the air. She has a tail! She is a mermaid. You've heard about mermaids living deep on the ocean floors, but you've never seen one up close.

The sun lowers beneath the horizon, and it starts to get dark. Soon the wind picks up. It becomes harder to hear the mermaid over the crashing waves. Then it starts to rain. The waves get bigger and more dangerous. You know it's not safe to stay. You hope the mermaid will be okay. Just as you are about to leave, you see a huge wave toss the mermaid toward some rocks on the beach.

You run to help her. Waves pummel the beach. Rain slashes through the air and stings your body. Up ahead, you see the mermaid lying on the sand. When you get to her, you can see she's hurt. Blood trickles down her forehead. You have to move fast. You grab under her arms and wade out into the ocean. You see a cove along the spit of land. It'll give some protection from the storm.

You wait with the mermaid until she stops bleeding and comes to.

"What happened?" she asks.

You tell her about the wave that tossed her against the rocks. "I brought you back into the water," you say.

"Thank you," she says, and smiles.

She says her name is Ariana Ponde. You stay in the cove with Ariana as the storm rages around you. She tells you about her home under the waves. You tell her about your travels. When the storm finally dies down, Ariana says she has to go.

"My family will be worried," she says.

You say goodbye, and she slips under the dark water and disappears.

Turn the page.

You loved having someone to talk to. Is that what it's like to have a friend? You return to the beach every day and talk with Ariana. Eventually you become close friends. She tells you more about her life as a mermaid. It sounds perfect.

"I wish I could live under the sea," you say.

One day, you visit your grandmother. You tell her all about your friend, the mermaid. You say how much you want to live in the water. Your grandmother smiles and takes your hand.

"If that is something you really want, I know someone who can help you," your grandmother says. She tells you about an old sea witch who lives near town. The witch has the power to grant wishes. "But," your grandmother warns, "her magic comes at a price."

80

To visit the sea witch, go to page 81.
To ask Ariana for help instead, turn to page 85.

The witch's home is at the edge between the ocean and rain forest. But it is not beautiful like either of those places. Instead, the area is infused with death.

It was a beautiful, sunny day when you started your journey. But it grows darker and colder the closer you get to the witch's house. As you walk the jagged stone path, you take note of all the dead, black trees and plants around. Skulls and other bones lie in piles. Smoke hangs in the air.

You reach the sea witch's house and knock on the door. It creaks open.

"Come in," says a voice.

You step inside. There, sitting in a chair made of bones, is the sea witch. Her black hair covers her pale face. Her red lips are pulled up in a grin.

Turn the page.

"So you want to live with the mer-people," she cackles. A shiver runs down your spine. You never told her your wish.

"I can make a potion," the sea witch continues. "It will let you live underwater."

"Yes, yes," you cry. "Give it to me!"

"Not so fast," the sea witch says, leaning forward in her chair. "My spells come at a cost."

"How much?" you ask.

"It is different for everyone," the witch says. She gets up and slinks closer to you. You can't help but step back. "Your price will be your voice."

"My, my voice?" you ask.

"Yes, your voice," says the witch. "Anytime you try to talk, you'll just burp up onions!"

"That doesn't sound *that* bad," you say.

"I'm not finished," she says, leaning in. "The little mermaid's family must accept you as one of their own. If they do not, the spell will come to an end. Your gills will disappear. Your fish tail will turn back into legs, and you will drown."

The witch holds out her wrinkled hand. "Do we have a deal?"

To take the sea witch's potion, turn to page 87.
To turn her down, turn to page 90.

The sea witch sounds unbelievable—and terrifying. You decide to see if Ariana can help.

The next day, you go to the beach and wait. It is a nice morning. You close your eyes and enjoy the sun. Soon, you hear Ariana singing. You stand up, clamber down to the water, and wave. She swims up to you.

"That was a beautiful song," you say, frowning.

"Thank you," Ariana says. "But what is the matter? You look sad."

"Ariana," you say, "You're my best friend—my only friend. I'm lonely when you're not here."

"You are my best friend too," Ariana says with a smile. "You must spend more time here."

"It is not enough. I want to be like you," you say. "Is there a way?"

Turn the page.

Ariana shakes her head. "I don't know. My parents have magical powers. But they've never used them on a human before."

"But if they use their magic on me, I won't be human anymore," you plead.

"I don't think it's a good idea," Ariana says.

You are certain that becoming a mer-person would make your life better. The only question is how do you do it?

86

To go back and try the sea witch, turn to page 92.
To beg Ariana to talk to her family, turn to page 94.

"Give me the potion," you say.

The sea witch cackles and rubs her hands together with joy. "Let's get to work!"

She pulls a big metal cauldron off of a shelf. She scrubs it clean with a fistful of snakes. They angrily hiss at her.

"Cleanliness is very important," the witch says, whistling a little tune while she scrubs.

Soon the sea witch is filling the cauldron with water and herbs. She adds some frog slime, stirs in some turtle tears, and mashes up some fish guts. She mumbles some magic words while **87** stirring. After it cooks for a few minutes, she dips a ladle into the pot and pours the bubbling potion into a glass.

"Drink up!" the witch smiles.

Turn the page.

It tastes awful. You can barely keep it down.

"Now," the sea witch says, "go to the ocean and dive into the water. Swim out far from the land."

"Dive in the ocean?" you ask, confused. "But I'll drown!"

"Trust the potion," the sea witch says. "You'll be a little fishy in no time."

You do as you are told. You go to the ocean's edge, close your eyes, and dive in. You swim as far as you can. When you can barely see the land behind you, you feel something happening.

Your legs have trouble kicking. They are stuck together!

"It's working," you try to say, but nothing comes out. You inhale and let out a big *BURP!* The stinky smell of onions is powerful. It makes your eyes water.

Finally you say, "RRR-IT'S WORKING."

You can feel gills growing into your neck. You dive down. You can breathe in water! You kick your tail. Soon, Ariana is swimming next to you. She has a big smile on her face.

"You made it!" she says. "But why does everything smell like onions? Gross."

Ariana's right. Even underwater, your breath reeks of onions. This may be more of a problem than you thought.

To try talking to Ariana, turn to page 96.
To keep your mouth shut and swim, turn to page 99.

You would love to swim with the mer-people under the sea. But the witch's price is too great. What if the potion doesn't work? What if Ariana's family doesn't accept you? You could die!

You leave the sea witch's home and run as fast as you can out of the evil forest. You go directly to the beach and out onto the rocks where Ariana is waiting. You tell her what happened.

"That sounds scary," Ariana says. She thinks for a minute. Then she swims out into the distance and disappears under the water.

The next day, you go out on the spit to meet Ariana. But she doesn't show up. She isn't there the next day either. You go out on the third day, but she doesn't come to meet you. You start to think you've lost your only friend.

As you are about to leave, you see someone waving to you on the beach. As she gets closer, you see a familiar smile. It's Ariana. But she's not a mermaid. She is standing on two legs!

"What?" you stammer. "How? Are you—?"

"Yes, I'm human!" she exclaims. "I went to see the sea witch instead. Now I can live on land with my best friend."

You hug her. You can't wait to take Ariana to Waterville to meet your family. And then who knows? You can go anywhere you want—except under the sea.

THE END

To follow another path, turn to page 9.

You return home looking for your grandmother. She must know how to find the sea witch. But when you walk inside, your family is waiting for you in the kitchen.

"There you are!" your father says with a sigh.

"Oh, thank goodness you're safe!" your grandmother exclaims. "I was afraid you made a deal with the sea witch."

"When I heard that you were asking about magic, I got worried," your father says. "That witch and her spells are not the answer."

You know that your father is right. You start to cry. Your brothers and sisters get up and put their arms around you.

Your oldest brother says, "We know you are lonely. But we are all here for you. I'm sorry if you didn't know it before."

At that moment, you know how lucky you really are. Your family loves you. They support you. You can't believe you almost left them. You don't wish to live under the sea anymore. That night, you have dinner with your family. You laugh and tell stories.

You continue to visit Ariana at the beach. Sometimes you even take your brothers and sisters with you. Eventually you make new friends—the human kind. One day you bring your friend, Sebastian, to the water to meet Ariana. While Sebastian and Ariana talk, you stare out into the water and think of the sea witch. You are so glad you didn't let her change who you are.

THE END

To follow another path, turn to page 9.

"Please talk to your parents," you beg Ariana.

"I don't know . . . ," Ariana says.

"Bring them here," you plead. "I can convince them!"

Ariana plunges into the water. A while later, she comes back with an adult mermaid and merman. "Meet my mom and dad," she says.

"Pleased to meet you," you say. And then you make your case. "Ariana and I are best friends. She always says how wonderful it is to live under the water. I want to live there too. Please help me. I want to be like you."

Ariana's father puts his hand on your shoulder. Her mother says, "You may think the answer to your problems is to become something else. But you are not meant to live with us. You are human. Your home is here."

You are crushed. Sad and frustrated, you go home. The next day, you return to the beach to meet Ariana. But your conversations have changed. You don't laugh with your friend anymore. All you can talk about is becoming a mer-person. Soon, Ariana stops meeting you at the beach. You've pushed your only friend away.

One day you are lying alone in the sun. You hear singing. You look around. It's not coming from the ocean. It's coming from the sky. A bird flies overhead. It lands in a tree on the beach. You follow it and listen. Its voice is amazing.

Forget the sea, you think. *The sky is where I want to be!*

Maybe the sea witch can turn you into a bird instead.

THE END
To follow another path, turn to page 9.

You're being silly. Ariana won't care if you smell like onions. You explain the situation.

"BLAH-SORRY ABOUT THE ONIONS," you belch in her face. IT'S A PPPPPP-ARRRRRT OF THE SPELL."

"Wow," Ariana says. "That's really awful."

She leads you to the deepest crevasse in the ocean, where her family lives. Her parents are waiting for you.

You burp, "PPPPPLLLAAAA-EASED TO MEET YOU." The heavy stench of onions is overwhelming.

Ariana's mother frowns. "That's quite a smell!"

Her father pinches his nose. "*You* are Ariana's friend? How dare you come here burping and stinking! Where are your manners? I think you should go home."

You swim away. Ariana's parents will never accept you as one of them. You realize this was the sea witch's plan all along. You feel foolish. Soon, the spell will wear off.

Suddenly a boat appears above you. You see people peering into the water. It's your brothers and sisters. You climb onto the boat. To your shock, you see that all of them are bald!

"We gave the sea witch our hair," says one of your brothers. "She told us how to save you. All you have to do is make Ariana cry. Her tears will break your spell. Then you can come home!"

98

Ariana is your friend. You couldn't make her cry. Can you? It may be the only way to save yourself.

To try to make your best friend cry, turn to page 101.

To say no, turn to page 103.

Ariana was *not* impressed by your onion burps. You doubt her parents will be either. You decide to keep quiet. You swim around as fast as you can. You do loops and spins. You squeeze through a coral tunnel. You explore a cave. Ariana joins you, and you both have a great time. Soon she has to go home. She invites you to join her.

When you arrive, Ariana introduces you to her mom and dad. They are friendly and ask lots of questions about your life on land. But you don't say anything in response. You don't want to stink them out. Instead, you smile and nod.

"Are you okay?" Ariana's mother asks.

"Won't you speak to us?" Ariana's father asks.

Turn the page.

You put your hands on your throat to tell them you can't talk. They seem to understand.

"Oh, I'm so sorry," Ariana's mother says.

You spend the rest of the day with Ariana and her family. They sing and laugh. You wish you could join in. It's not as fun as you hoped it would be to live down here.

During dinner, they invite you to stay in their underwater community. You are so happy! You wish you could thank them, but you don't dare open your mouth. You spend the rest of your days living a quiet life under the sea.

THE END

To follow another path, turn to page 9.

You just want your old life back. Ariana will understand. Your siblings wait in the boat while you call out for Ariana. When she comes, she gives you a smile and starts to sing.

"ST-OOOP!" you belch. "IIII'D RATHER SMMMMELL LIKE OOOONIONS FOR-EEEVER THAN HEAR YOOUR TERRIBLE VOICE OONE MORE TIIIME."

Ariana freezes, then a deep frown spreads across her face. A single tear falls from her eyes and lands in the sea.

"Don't worry, you never have to hear me sing again," Ariana says angrily. Then she swims away. You feel terrible.

Turn the page.

"IIIII'M SO-O-O-RRRY," you belch after her. But she doesn't answer back.

"Ariana, I didn't mean what I said!" you yell. But this time, you don't belch. You don't burp. You sound like yourself again! You crawl into the boat with your family. You're so happy to be alive. But you hurt your best—and only—friend. You never see Ariana again.

THE END

To follow another path, turn to page 9.

"BRRR-I CAAAN'T DO THAT," you burp.

You can't hurt your best friend. She was there for you when no one else was. You wave goodbye to your siblings and lay back in the water. Your body loses feeling as you begin to sink to the bottom of the ocean.

But then something strange happens. A hand reaches up from the bottom of the sea and grabs you. You open your eyes. It's Ariana's mother. Her father is on your other side. You look down. Your whole body is glowing. You start to float in the water. Slowly, your skin turns green. Your fingers sprout small leaves. You are not a mermaid anymore. But you're not human either. You've been turned into a beautiful sea plant.

103

Turn the page.

You spend the rest of your days in the ocean. Though you can't swim, you sway freely with the shifting currents. Colorful fish swim by. Other plants seem to dance with the moving water. Sometimes you can even see the sun's rays twinkle high above on the water's surface.

You miss your family. But as the days go by, you think of them less and less. Pretty soon you forget all about your life on land.

THE END

To follow another path, turn to page 9.

CHAPTER 5

THE LITTLE MERMAID THROUGH HISTORY

Hans Christian Andersen published "The Little Mermaid" in 1837. It was part of a collection of tales called *Fairy Tales Told for Children*. In Andersen's version, a little mermaid swims to the sea's surface on her fifteenth birthday. There, she sees a prince celebrating his birthday on a ship.

During the night, a storm destroys the ship. The prince is thrown into the ocean. The little mermaid saves the prince and drags him to land. Afterward, the mermaid longs to see the prince again. She loves him. She meets a witch who agrees to make her human.

In exchange, the mermaid gives away her voice. She must also get the prince to fall in love with her. If not, the mermaid will die.

The prince finds the mermaid. They become close friends. But the prince does not fall in love with her. He marries someone else. The little mermaid knows she will die.

On the night of the prince's wedding, the little mermaid sees her five older sisters in the water. They have given their hair to the witch in exchange for a knife. They tell the little mermaid to kill her beloved prince with it. That will break the witch's spell.

The mermaid refuses to kill the prince, and she dies. But her spirit is transformed. The little mermaid becomes a daughter of the air. Her spirit lives on for the next 300 years, helping others.

The story's ending was very important to Andersen. In fact, the original title for the fairy tale was "Daughters of the Air." Andersen wanted the little mermaid to choose her own path in life and death.

"The Little Mermaid" has become an important part of our culture. The story has been retold for generations in comic books, novels, and art. It has also been shown in plays, TV shows, and movies.

The most well-known version of the story is the 1989 Disney animated movie, *The Little Mermaid*. In it, the little mermaid is named Ariel. Her sea friends Sebastian, Scuttle, and Flounder help Ariel try to win Prince Eric's heart. The movie won two Academy Awards. One was for the song "Under the Sea."

Other Paths to Explore

1. In chapter 3, the main character wishes to be part of another group. Have you ever felt that way? What did you do?

2. In the original fairy tale, the sea witch makes the little mermaid give up her voice. Why do you think the witch chose this price?

3. Read the original version of "The Little Mermaid." How is the story different from other versions you've heard? How is it the same?

Read More

Gish, Ashley. *Mermaids.* Mankato, MN: Creative Education, 2020.

Hile, Lori. *Mermaids: Myth or Reality?* North Mankato, MN: Capstone Press, 2019.

Laskow, Sarah. *The Very Short, Entirely True History of Mermaids.* Penguin Workshop, 2020.

Internet Sites

From Mermaids to Manatees: The Myth and the Reality
https://ocean.si.edu/ocean-life/marine-mammals/mermaids-manatees-myth-and-reality

The Little Mermaid
https://andersen.sdu.dk/vaerk/hersholt/TheLittleMermaid_e.html

Mermaids & Mermen: Facts & Legends
https://www.livescience.com/39882-mermaid.html

LOOK FOR OTHER BOOKS IN THIS SERIES:

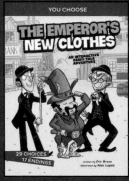